2019?

PUFFIN BOOK

D0476418

THE WITCH'S DOG AND THE TALKING PICTURE

Frank Rodgers has written and illustrated a wide range of books for children: picture books, storybooks, non-fiction and novels. His children's stories have been broadcast on radio and TV and he created a sitcom series for CBBC based on his book *The Intergalactic Kitchen.* His recent work for Puffin includes the Eyetooth books and the bestselling Witch's Dog, and Robodog titles. He was an art teacher before becoming an author and illustrator and lives in Glasgow with his wife. He has two grown-up children.

Frank Rodgers

The Witch's Dog and the Talking Picture

PUFFIN

PUFFIN BOOKS

Published by the Penguin Group
Penguin Books Ltd, 80 Strand, London WC2R 0RL, England
Penguin Group (USA) Inc., 375 Hudson Street, New York, New York 10014, USA
Penguin Group (Canada), 90 Eglinton Avenue East, Suite 700, Toronto, Ontario,
Canada M4P 2Y3 (a division of Pearson Penguin Canada Inc.)
Penguin Ireland, 25 St Stephen's Green, Dublin 2, Ireland (a division of Penguin Books Ltd)
Penguin Group (Australia), 250 Camberwell Road, Camberwell, Victoria 3124, Australia
(a division of Pearson Australia Group Pty Ltd)
Penguin Books India Pvt Ltd, 11 Community Centre, Panchsheel Park,
New Delhi – 110 017, India
Penguin Group (NZ), cnr Airborne and Rosedale Roads, Albany, Auckland 1310,
New Zealand (a division of Pearson New Zealand Ltd)
Penguin Books (South Africa) (Pty) Ltd, 24 Sturdee Avenue, Rosebank,
Johannesburg 2196, South Africa

Penguin Books Ltd, Registered Offices: 80 Strand, London WC2R 0RL, England

www.penguin.com

First published 2006
1

Copyright © Frank Rodgers, 2006
All rights reserved

The moral right of the author/illustrator has been asserted

Typeset in Times New Roman Infant
Printed in China by Midas Printing Ltd

Except in the United States of America, this book is sold subject to the condition that it
shall not, by way of trade or otherwise, be lent, re-sold, hired out, or otherwise circulated
without the publisher's prior consent in any form of binding or cover other than that in
which it is published and without a similar condition including this condition being
imposed on the subsequent purchaser

British Library Cataloguing in Publication Data
A CIP catalogue record for this book is available from the British Library

ISBN-13: 987-0-141-31814-1
ISBN-10: 0-141-31814-7

MORAY COUNCIL LIBRARIES· & INFO.SERVICES	
2O 19 39 37	
Askews	
JB	

Wilf, the witch's dog, was
painting a picture of Weenie
casting a spell.
The picture was for the Witches'
Pets' Painting Show . . . and Wilf
was having a bit of bother with it.

"Can't you keep still, Weenie?" he
asked. "Please? It's like trying to
paint a jumping bean."

"I'm sorry, Wilf," apologized
Weenie. "It's just that I'm wondering
where Aunt Bella might be. She's the
guest of honour today because she's
a famous painter . . .

but I haven't seen
her lately. She seems
to have disappeared.

Those pictures of hers
are meant to be in the show."

"Don't worry," Wilf said. "She's
probably off somewhere painting
and has forgotten."
"I'm sure you're right, Wilf," sighed
Weenie, fidgeting again.

Wilf sighed too. "The painting show begins soon and my picture isn't finished," he said. "I still haven't painted the spell shooting out from your fingertips, Weenie."

"Oh dear. It's my fault, Wilf," said Weenie.

"And look, it's too late now. We
must go right away or we'll be late."

"Never mind," said Wilf. "I'll
bring my paints and brushes to the
show. Maybe I'll get a chance to
finish my painting before it starts."

As Weenie helped Wilf put his
painting into its frame, a strange
thing happened.

Behind them another of Aunt Bella's
paintings suddenly appeared out of
nowhere.

It was a portrait of
a queen and it
hovered in the air for
a few seconds . . .

before quietly
gliding down to
join the pictures
that stood against
the wall.

Neither Wilf nor Weenie noticed this. They didn't even spot the new picture when Wilf's friends arrived to help carry the paintings to the village hall.

"I'll take the heaviest ones," said Bertie, flexing his muscles.

"And we'll help Wilf
carry the rest," said
Harry and Streaky.

"I'll just pop round to Aunt Bella's
house to see if she's back,"
said Weenie anxiously. "See
you all at the show."

At the village hall the witches' pets
were hanging up their paintings. It
was a very colourful display.

Sly Cat and Tricky
Toad slouched against
a pillar.
"I forgot to do a painting . . ."
muttered Tricky, "on purpose."

Sly smirked. "I didn't." He held up a
white sheet of paper.
"This is my picture."
"But there's nothing
there," said
Tricky, puzzled.

"Yes there is," Sly sniggered.
"It's my painting of an iceberg in a
blizzard."
"Iceberg in a blizzard!" giggled
Tricky. "That's a good one, Sly!"

Sly grinned . . . then glowered as he
saw Wilf's painting.
He and Tricky had always been
jealous of Wilf.

"Wilf's picture of Weenie looks
good," said Tricky with a frown.
"Even though it's not finished."

Sly glowered even more.
"It'll be finished when I'm through
with it," he muttered nastily.

He pulled Tricky
out of sight
behind the
pillar.

"Let's see if we can make it fly
away!" he hissed.

Wilf hung his painting on the wall,
and then his friends helped him to
hang Aunt Bella's pictures.

"I like that painting of a queen,"
remarked Harry.

"Yes," said Wilf thoughtfully. "It's
very good but I can't remember
seeing it before. Isn't that strange?"

At that moment Sly and Tricky's
spell hit Wilf's painting.

The picture wobbled,
then suddenly shot into
the air.

"What's going on?"
cried Wilf in
surprise.

Behind the pillar,
Sly and Tricky
giggled.
"Your picture's
going to fly out of
the window, that's
what's going on,"
tittered Sly.

But it didn't.

Wilf's painting just
stayed there, floating
in the air.

"We didn't make the spell strong
enough!" groaned Tricky.
All of a sudden Wilf's painting fell
. . . knocking the picture of the
queen to the floor
as it went.

Sly and Tricky
dodged back out of
sight just as Weenie
arrived . . . still
without her Aunt Bella.

"What happened, Wilf?" Weenie cried.

"I think somebody tried a spell out on my painting, Weenie," replied Wilf. "It jumped off the wall and bumped into this picture. But they're both all right."

Weenie sighed.

"Aunt Bella's nowhere to be found and now there are strange spells about. Oh dear."

Bertie looked around suspiciously but didn't see Sly or Tricky.

As Wilf put his own picture back on the wall, Weenie picked up the painting of the queen.

"Look at this,"
she said.
"There's a bit
of paper with
writing on it
stuck to the
back of this
picture. It looks
like a spell."

Weenie removed the piece of paper,
peered at it and gasped.

"It's from
Aunt Bella!"
she cried. "It
says . . . 'Use
this spell
immediately!'"

"You must do it, Weenie," said Wilf urgently. "It might be something to do with your aunt's disappearance!"

Weenie nodded.
"I know," she replied. "Right, here goes . . ."

Carefully she read out the spell . . .

but nothing seemed to happen.
"Perhaps I didn't read it properly,"
said Weenie.

"You did," said a sudden voice behind
them. "You read it perfectly well."

Everyone spun round . . . but no one
was there.

"Who said
that?" asked
Streaky,
puzzled.

"Me," said the voice.
Everybody stared at Aunt Bella's
picture in amazement.
It was the painted queen who
was talking!

"There's no time to lose," the queen
went on. "Your Aunt Bella needs
your help, Weenie. She was trying out
some magic travel dust and managed
to send herself back in time . . .

to my castle. Now she can't get
home again. She only had enough
magic dust left to send this painting
of me secretly to your house."

Weenie gasped.

"I've got plenty of magic travel dust," she cried. "But it's in my kitchen!"

"I'll get it!" Streaky cried.

Weenie quickly told Streaky where it was and off he zoomed.

"Back in a tick!" he called.

Behind the pillar Tricky frowned.
"Talking pictures," he muttered.
"Whatever next?"

"Never mind," hissed Sly. "It's given
me an idea. We're going to paint a
much better picture than Wilf."

"How are we going to do that?" asked Tricky.
"By magic," sniggered Sly.

Peering out, he saw that no one was looking his way. Sneakily he reached out, took hold of the bag containing Wilf's paints and brushes and quickly pulled it behind the pillar.

A moment later Streaky dashed
back into the hall, hardly out of
breath.

"Here you are,
Weenie," he
declared,
giving her the
box of magic
travel dust.

"Thank you, Streaky," cried Weenie.
She took out a small handful of the
sparkling dust.

"Now . . . I'm off
to see Aunt Bella!"

"I'll go with you, Weenie," said Wilf.

"And don't forget me," added the
queen. "I know the way!"
Wilf took the picture off the wall
and Weenie sprinkled the magic
travel dust over them.

"Here goes,"
she said,
and recited
a spell.

There was a sudden FLASH!
and Weenie, Wilf and the talking
picture disappeared.
They shot back in time . . .

tumbling over and over until . . .
BUMP . . . they landed in a corner
of the great hall of a castle.

"We're here!" said the queen in the
picture. "Look . . . there's me!"
Weenie and Wilf looked. On the other
side of the hall the actual queen sat
on her throne beside the king.
Around them were their courtiers.

"There's Aunt Bella!"
cried Weenie.

Her aunt was standing
in front of an easel
beside the king's throne with her
brushes in her hands.

"Bella's painting my husband now,"
remarked the queen in the picture.
"That's nice."

"You are such a good painter,
madam," said the king. "You must
stay here until you have painted the
entire court."

"Yes, you must," agreed his wife.
"That is a Royal Proclamation!"

"But . . ." protested Aunt Bella, "that means I'll be stuck here for ages!"

"We have spoken!" declared the queen haughtily. "You will stay!"

"That's not very fair, is it?" said the queen in the picture to Wilf and Weenie. "I'm going to have a word with myself about this!"

But Wilf shook his head.

"I've got a good idea," he whispered.

"What we need to do is distract the king and queen," Wilf went on.

"Then Aunt Bella can sneak away with Weenie and me without a fuss."

He looked at the queen in the painting. "Will you help me?"

"I will," replied the talking picture. "It <u>is</u> a good idea!"

"Wonderful!" said Wilf. "Don't say a word until I give you a wink, OK?"

"OK," answered the queen. "This is exciting!"

"Good luck, Wilf," whispered Weenie.

Wilf marched into the middle of the
great hall, holding the painting in
front of him.
Everyone turned towards him in
astonishment.

"Who are you?" asked the king.
"And what are you doing with my
picture?" demanded the queen.

"My name is Wilf, the witch's dog," replied Wilf. "And I've come to show you some magic!"

"Magic?" cried the king, interested. "What kind of magic?"

"Yes, what kind of magic?" asked the queen. "Is it something to do with my painting?"

"It is," Wilf declared. "Now . . . watch!" He propped the picture against a pillar and pretended to aim a spell at it. "Abracadabra . . . hey presto!" he exclaimed, winking at the painting.

"You are now a talking picture!"

The painted queen winked back . . .
then smiled at the queen on the
throne.

"Hello, me," she said. "I must say
you look as pretty as a picture . . .
this picture!" She laughed merrily as
everyone gasped in amazement.

"My painting talks!" exclaimed the queen. I have a talking picture!" She clapped her hands in delight. "Now I can have a conversation with the most interesting person in the castle . . .

myself! Just what I've always wanted."

"I'm so pleased," said the king.

He and the queen leapt from their thrones and joined the throng of excited courtiers.

Wilf gave the painting to the queen, who gazed at her own face in delight.

As everyone crowded closer to hear the queen talk to herself, Wilf slipped away with Aunt Bella.

Weenie was waiting for them by the
door. She was overjoyed to see her
aunt.

"Thank you both for coming!" Aunt
Bella whispered gratefully.

"We'd better go before the king and
queen remember about me!"

Quickly Weenie sprinkled some
magic travel dust over them and
recited the spell.

There was a bright blue

and they disappeared . . .

just as the king and queen turned round.

"Oh dear!" said the king. "Bella's gone and she hasn't finished my portrait."

"Bother!" cried the queen.

"Actually," said the talking picture, "there's a painter I've heard about called Leonardo da Vinci."

"In that case," replied the queen, "we'll get him to finish it."

"Leonardo da Vinci?" grumbled the king. "Never heard of him. I hope he's as good as Bella."

In the village hall Sly was in the act of putting a spell on Wilf's paints and brushes.

"These will come alive just like the painting did," he whispered to Tricky. "Then I'll get them to paint a wonderful picture for me . . . much better than Wilf's!"

"Much better!" agreed Tricky gleefully.

Swiftly Sly sent out the spell. It
crackled around the paints and
brushes . . .

but, as well as making them come
alive, it made them grow bigger.

MUCH bigger!

"Oh, no!" yelped Sly as the huge brushes dipped themselves in the paints. "My spell has gone wrong!"

"Run!" cried Tricky.

A big blob of blue paint whizzed over his head and splattered against the door.

Harry, Bertie, Streaky and the
witches' pets scattered as the brushes
swept around the room . . .

throwing splashes of bright colour
everywhere.

SPLISH

The walls were
splattered with red
and yellow.

SPLASH

The windows
were sprayed
with blue and
green.

SPLOSH

The floor was
showered with
purple and pink.

Suddenly Weenie, Wilf and Aunt Bella
appeared in a puff of magic dust.

"Help!" wailed Sly and Tricky as
they rushed past, chased by two
enormous brushes. "Do something!"

Quickly Weenie, Aunt Bella and
Wilf sent out spells.

Wilf's giant jumping paints and
brushes were returned to normal . . .
but not before Sly and
Tricky had been
covered in paint
from head to foot.

"Serves you right!" said the Head Teacher, who had been told about what was happening.

"Now go and get washed, then come back and clean this entire hall!"

Sly and Tricky slunk away miserably.

"Oh dear," said the Head Teacher when she saw the pictures. "The paintings are ruined. The show will have to be cancelled."

"Don't worry," replied Aunt Bella. "I know a special spell which will sort them out. It's very handy being a painter and a witch, you know!"

Wilf looked at his own painting and grinned.

"As long as you don't sort out my painting," he said. "Look what my wild paints have done.

They've finished off my picture for me!"

Everyone looked at Wilf's painting
and smiled.

"So they have!" exclaimed Weenie.
"Look, my spell has been coloured
in! The painting looks terrific."

"It certainly does,"
said the Head
Teacher.
"Thank you," said
Wilf.

"What kind of spell is Weenie
making in your picture, Wilf?" asked
Aunt Bella curiously, peering at
Wilf's painting.

"Yes, Wilf," said
Weenie. "What
kind is it?"

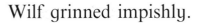

Wilf grinned impishly.
"A spell you've never used, Weenie –
but one that your aunt could
show you," he replied. "It's
a queen's favourite. The
kind of spell that changes
an ordinary painting . . .

into a talking picture!"